Let Me
Hold You Longer

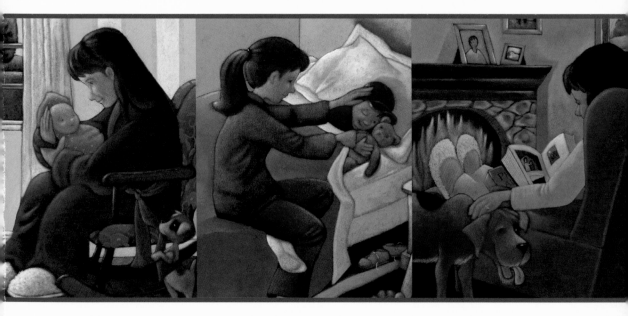

WRITTEN BY BESTSELLING AUTHOR

KAREN KINGSBURY
ILLUSTRATED BY MARY COLLIER

TYNDALE HOUSE PUBLISHERS   CAROL STREAM, ILLINOIS

DEDICATED TO

Donald, my best friend
Kelsey, my sweet laughter
Tyler, my forever song
Sean, my silly heart
Josh, my gentle giant
EJ, my first chosen
Austin, my miracle boy
And to God Almighty,
who has—for now—blessed me with these

Visit Tyndale's website for kids at tyndale.com/kids.

TYNDALE and Tyndale's quill logo are registered trademarks of Tyndale House Ministries. The Tyndale Kids Logo is a trademark of Tyndale House Ministries.

Let Me Hold You Longer

The material in this book is based on the poem "Would I Have Held on Longer?" taken from the text of a novel titled *Rejoice,* coauthored by Karen Kingsbury and Gary Smalley.

Designed by Julie Chen

Edited by Betty Free Swanberg

Published in association with the literary agency of Alive Communications, Inc., 7680 Goddard Street, Suite 200, Colorado Springs, CO 80920.

For manufacturing information regarding this product, please call 1-800-323-9400.

For information about special discounts for bulk purchases, please contact Tyndale House Publishers at csresponse@tyndale.com, or call 1-800-323-9400.

ISBN 978-1-4143-8987-5

Printed in the United States of America

26 25 24 23 22 21 20
12 11 10   9   8   7   6

A NOTE FROM THE AUTHOR

Not long ago my little son Austin ran to me, jumped into my arms, and wrapped his legs around my waist. We rubbed noses and he whispered into my ear, "I love you, Mommy."

Then he slid down and ran to play.

As he left, I realized that he was almost too big, too heavy for me to hold him that way. I looked outside at my oldest son, Tyler, on the verge of middle school, and I thought back. At some point Tyler ran to me and jumped into my arms like that for the last time.

The very last time.

And that's when it hit me. We spend our children's days celebrating their firsts. First step, first tooth, first words. First day of kindergarten, first homecoming dance, first time behind the wheel. But somehow, along the way, we miss their lasts.

There are no photographs or parties when a child takes his last nap or catches tadpoles for the last time. For the most part, it's impossible to know when a last-moment actually occurs. Nothing signals a mother to stop and notice the last time her little boy runs and jumps into her arms the way Austin—for now—still does.

Then I wondered a bit more, and Tyler came to mind again. Would I have held on longer if I'd known it was the last time? And so I began to write. Sometimes with tears in my eyes, I chronicled the life of a child and all the last times we might miss along the way.

In the process, my first children's book was born.

The beautiful illustrations in *Let Me Hold You Longer* are fun and lighthearted—so that your children will laugh and giggle while you quietly ponder the speed of life. This is a book for kids, a gift for graduates, a treasure for anyone who has ever loved a child.

Most of all, it is a labor of love from me—a mom of six kids who knows all too well the short time we have with our little ones.

Long ago you came to me,
    a miracle of firsts:
First smiles and teeth and baby steps,
    a sunbeam on the burst.
But one day you will move away
    and leave to me your past,
And I will be left thinking of
    a lifetime of your lasts . . .

The last time that I held a bottle
to your baby lips.
The last time that I lifted you
and held you on my hip.

The last night when you woke up crying,
    needing to be walked,
When last you crawled up with your blanket,
    wanting to be rocked.

The last time when you ran to me,
　　still small enough to hold.
The last time that you said you'd marry
　　me when you grew old.
Precious, simple moments and
　　bright flashes from your past—
Would I have held on longer if
　　I'd known they were your last?

Our last adventure to the park,
  your final midday nap,
The last time when you wore your favorite
  faded baseball cap.

Your last few hours of kindergarten,
those last days of first grade,
Your last at bat in Little League,
last colored picture made.

I never said good-bye to all
    your yesterdays long passed.
So what about tomorrow—
    will I recognize your lasts?

The last time that you catch a frog
 in that old backyard pond.
The last time that you run barefoot
 across our fresh-cut lawn.
Silly, scattered images
 will represent your past.
I keep on taking pictures,
 never quite sure of your lasts . . .

The last time that I comb your hair
   or stop a pillow fight.
The last time that I pray with you
   and tuck you in at night.
The last time when we cuddle
   with a book, just me and you.
The last time you jump in our bed
   and sleep between us two.

The last piano lesson,
last vacation to the lake.
Your last few weeks of middle school,
last soccer goal you make.

I look ahead and dream of days
that haven't come to pass.
But as I do, I sometimes miss
today's sweet, precious lasts . . .

The last time that I help you with
a math or spelling test.

The last time when I shout that yes,
  your room is still a mess.
The last time that you need me for
  a ride from here to there.
The last time that you spend the night
  with your old tattered bear.

My life keeps moving faster,
  stealing precious days that pass.
I want to hold on longer—
  want to recognize your lasts . . .

The last time that you need my help
with details of a dance.
The last time that you ask me for
advice about romance.

The last time that you talk to me
about your hopes and dreams.
The last time that you wear a jersey
for your high school team.

I've watched you grow and barely noticed
seasons as they pass.
If I could freeze the hands of time,
I'd hold on to your lasts.

For come some bright fall morning,
  you'll be going far away.
College life will beckon
  in a brilliant sort of way.
One last hug, one last good-bye,
  one quick and hurried kiss.
One last time to understand
  just how much you'll be missed.
I'll watch you leave and think how fast
  our time together passed.